Funny
Bunny Tales

Max &
Ruby

Grosset & Dunlap
An Imprint of Penguin Group (USA) Inc.

GROSSET & DUNLAP
Published by the Penguin Group
Penguin Group (USA) Inc., 375 Hudson Street, New York, New York 10014, USA
Penguin Group (Canada), 90 Eglinton Avenue East, Suite 700,
Toronto, Ontario M4P 2Y3, Canada
(a division of Pearson Penguin Canada Inc.)
Penguin Books Ltd., 80 Strand, London WC2R 0RL, England
Penguin Group Ireland, 25 St. Stephen's Green, Dublin 2, Ireland
(a division of Penguin Books Ltd.)
Penguin Group (Australia), 250 Camberwell Road, Camberwell, Victoria 3124, Australia
(a division of Pearson Australia Group Pty. Ltd.)
Penguin Books India Pvt. Ltd., 11 Community Centre, Panchsheel Park,
New Delhi—110 017, India
Penguin Group (NZ), 67 Apollo Drive, Rosedale, North Shore 0632, New Zealand
(a division of Pearson New Zealand Ltd.)
Penguin Books (South Africa) (Pty.) Ltd., 24 Sturdee Avenue,
Rosebank, Johannesburg 2196, South Africa

Penguin Books Ltd., Registered Offices:
80 Strand, London WC2R 0RL, England

Based upon the animated series Max & Ruby
A Nelvana Limited production © 2002–2003.

Max & Ruby™ and © Rosemary Wells. Licensed by Nelvana Limited NELVANA™ Nelvana Limited. CORUS™ Corus Entertainment Inc. All Rights Reserved. Used under license by Penguin Young Readers Group. Published in 2011 by Grosset & Dunlap, a division of Penguin Young Readers Group, 345 Hudson Street, New York, New York 10014. GROSSET & DUNLAP is a trademark of Penguin Group (USA) Inc. Manufactured in China.

ISBN 978-0-448-45534-1   10 9 8 7 6 5 4

Ruby's Pajama Party

It was the middle of the afternoon, and Ruby was wearing a fancy nightgown.

"Max, I'm having a pajama party," said Ruby. "All my friends are coming!"

Ruby showed Max the carrot cake nibbles she had made for the party.

Max tried to taste one.

"Max," said Ruby, "these are for my guests!"

Then the doorbell rang. Ruby's friends had arrived!

Max wanted to join the pajama party.
"Girls only, Max!" said Ruby.
Then Ruby and her friends went upstairs to her bedroom.

Ruby, Louise, and Valerie showed one another their pajamas.

They could not decide whose were prettiest.

So Max put on his pajamas and went to Ruby's room.
"No, Max," said Ruby. "This is a private pajama party!"
"We are going to do makeovers," said Louise. "Boys
don't do makeovers!"

Max peeked in the door while Ruby, Louise, and Valerie put on makeup.

Then he had an idea. He went into the bathroom and found a Hot Lips Lipstick.

Max put the lipstick all over his face. Then he showed the girls.

"Max, wash off that lipstick," said Ruby. "We're going to dance now. You should go play with your trucks."

But Max wanted to join the dance party.
So he came back with his windup, dancing chicks.
"Max!" said Ruby.

But the girls loved the dancing chicks.
"Okay, Max, you can stay for a little while," said Ruby.

All that dancing made Ruby and her friends hungry.
So Ruby went and got the carrot cake nibbles she
had made.

When Ruby came back, she saw that her friends had fallen asleep!
Dancing with the chicks had made them very tired.

"Who's going to eat all these snacks now?" asked Ruby.
"Me!" said Max.

Ruby's Hiccups

Max had lost his Wally the Werewolf mask. He wanted Ruby's help finding it.

"Not now, Max," said Ruby. "We are practicing for the Bunny Scout Talent Show. *HICCUP!*"

"Oh no," said Ruby. "I have the hiccups."
"How can we practice our song now?" asked Louise.

"I know," said Ruby. "*HICCUP!* Let's look up a cure in the *Big Book of Home Remedies*."

"Good idea," said Louise.

Ruby looked under *H* for *hiccups*. "It says that there are four—*HICCUP!*—cures for the hiccups. Hold your breath, turn upside down, drink a glass of water, and be scared," said Ruby.

First, Ruby tried holding her breath.
"Werewolf mask!" said Max.

"I don't know where—*HICCUP!*—your mask is," said Ruby. "Try looking in your sandbox, Max."

Max looked in the sandbox, but he didn't find his mask.

Meanwhile, Louise suggested that Ruby try hanging upside down.

"Did it work?" asked Louise.
"*HICCUP!*" said Ruby. "What am I going to do?"

"Werewolf mask!" said Max.
"I can't help you now, Max," said Ruby. "Try checking under your bed."

While Max went upstairs, Ruby drank some water.
Glug, glug, glug!
She hoped this would make her hiccups go away.

But the water didn't help, either!
"There's only one cure left," said Louise. "Maybe we should try it."
Just then, the doorbell rang.

"GRRR! AHHH!" growled a monster.
"Eeeek!" shouted Ruby. "A werewolf!"

But it was only Grandma wearing Max's mask.
"I hope I didn't scare you too much," said Grandma.
"Ruby!" cried Louise. "Being scared is the fourth way to get rid of the hiccups!"

"Did it work?" Louise asked.

"I'm not sure," said Ruby. She waited a few moments . . . and didn't hiccup once. "They're gone! Hooray!"

Max the Baby

Ruby and Louise wanted to be babysitters.
To get some practice, they were helping Mrs. Huffington with her baby.

Ruby and Louise rocked and sang to the baby.
"We have to be careful with a real baby," said Ruby.
"I know," said Louise. "He's not fake like a doll!"

Soon Mrs. Huffington said, "It's time to head home for nap time. Thank you for the help, girls!"
"What are we going to do now?" asked Ruby.

"We could babysit our doll," said Louise. "We have everything we need in our babysitting kit."

"It would be more fun to babysit a real baby," said Ruby.

"Let's get Max!" the girls cried.

Ruby put a bonnet on Max, but Max wanted to go play.
"No, Max," said Ruby.
"You're our baby now," said Louise.

"Baby, do you want to play with a rattle?" asked Ruby.
"Baby, do you want to play with this bear?" asked Louise.
"No baby!" said Max.

Next the girls tried to give Max a snack.
But Max would not eat it.

41

Max tried to crawl away.
"No baby!" said Max.

"A diaper! That's what the baby needs!" said Louise.
So the girls took a diaper out of their babysitting kit.
Max hated the diaper.

"Baby doesn't seem happy," said Ruby.
"Maybe he's sick!" said Louise.
While the girls looked in their baby book, Max crawled away.

"Max, you can't go down the slide," said Ruby. "The baby book says you have to take a nap."

"We will sing you a sleepy, sleepy lullaby," said Louise.

Max lay down on the bench between Ruby and Louise.
But as the girls sang the lullaby to Max, they got sleepy!
Babysitting was hard work.

In no time at all, Ruby and Louise fell asleep.
Max saw his chance to get away!

Max threw off all the baby clothes and went back to the slide.

"No baby!" shouted Max.